spot

CREEPY CRAWLIES

FLIES

by Nessa Black

AMICUS | AMICUS INK

eyes

feet

Look for these words and pictures as you read.

wings

mouth

Buzz! Buzz!

Here come a fly!

Flies are insects.
They live all over the world.
Have you ever seen one up close?

Look at its big eyes.
Many small eyes are in each one.
The fly can see things move.

eyes

feet

Look at its feet.
They are sticky.
A fly can hang upside down.

Look at its wings.
They are big. They are thin.
They can flap 200
times a second!

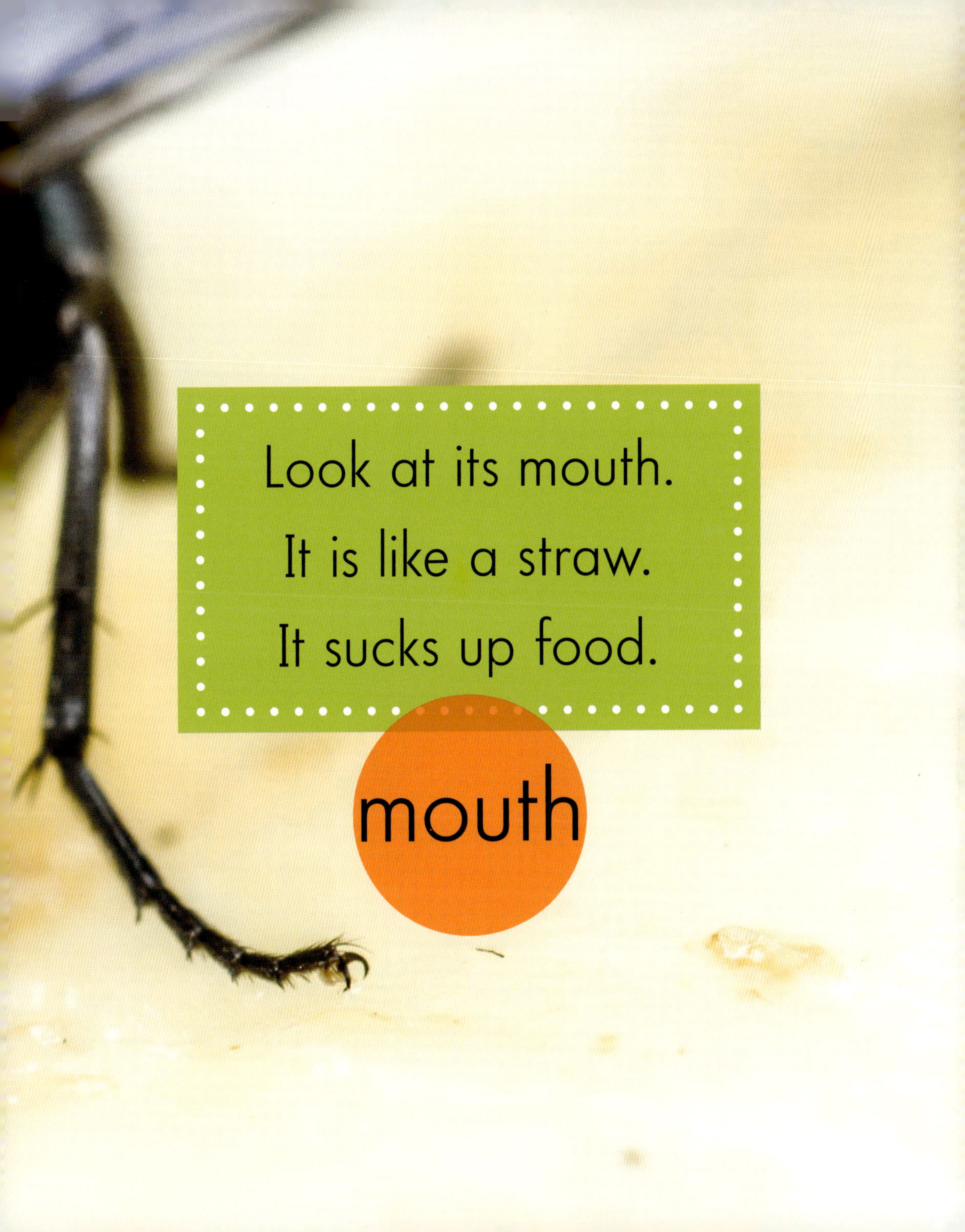

Look at its mouth.
It is like a straw.
It sucks up food.

Can you find all the flies?

Did you find?

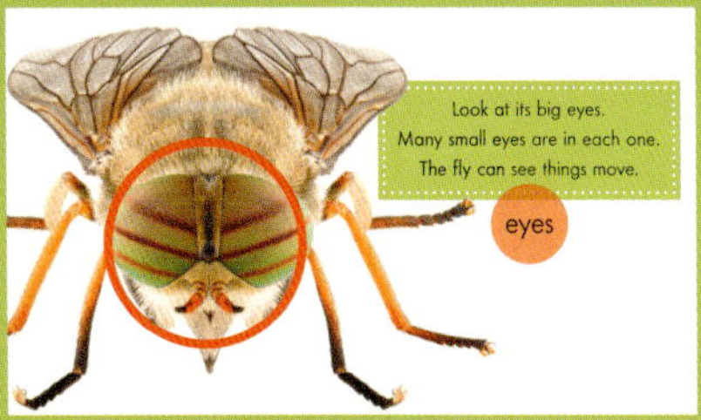

eyes

feet

wings

mouth

Spot is published by Amicus and Amicus Ink
P.O. Box 1329, Mankato, MN 56002
www.amicuspublishing.us

Library of Congress Cataloging-in-Publication Data
Names: Black, Nessa, author.
Title: Flies / by Nessa Black.
Description: Mankato, Minnesota : Amicus, [2018] | Series: Spot. Creepy crawlies | Audience: K to grade 3.
Identifiers: LCCN 2016055562| ISBN 9781681511085 (library binding) | ISBN 9781681522272 (pbk.) | ISBN 9781681511986 (e-book)
Subjects: LCSH: Flies--Juvenile literature.
Classification: LCC QL533.2 .B53 2018 | DDC 595.77--dc23
LC record available at https://lccn.loc.gov/2016055562

Printed in China

HC 10 9 8 7 6 5 4 3 2 1
PB 10 9 8 7 6 5 4 3 2 1

Wendy Dieker, editor
Deb Miner, series designer
Ciara Beitlich, book designer
Holly Young, photo researcher

Photos by AgeFotostock cover; Dreamstime 10–11; iStock 3; Shutterstock 1, 4–5, 6–7, 8–9, 10–11, 12–13, 14–15